Princess Katie's Kittens

Bella at the Ball

Princess Katie's Kittens

Collect all the kittens!

Julie Sykes

Princess Katie's Kittens

Bella at the Ball

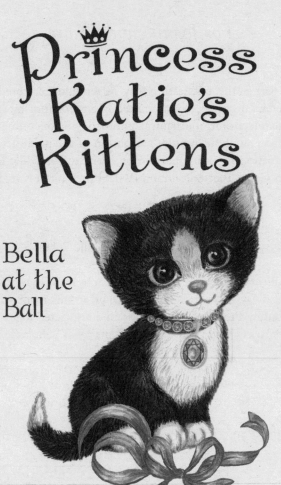

SCHOLASTIC INC.

For Joanne and Claire

ISBN 978-0-545-69221-2

Text copyright ©2012 by Julie Sykes

All rights reserved. Published by Scholastic Inc., 557 Broadway, New York, NY 10012, by arrangement with Piccadilly Press Ltd. SCHOLASTIC and associated logos are trademarks and/or registered trademarks of Scholastic Inc.

Cover design by Simon Davis
Cover illustration by Sue Hellard
Inside illustrations by Richard Morgan

12 11 10 9 8 7 6 5 4 3 2 1   14 15 16 17 18 19/0

Printed in the U.S.A.   40

First Scholastic printing, September 2014

Chapter 1

A Toy Mouse

Princess Katie of Tula and her best friend, Becky Philips, hurried down the palace hall toward the mudroom. They were on their way to see Princess Katie's kittens. It had been a whole week since Katie had found the six tiny cats abandoned in a box in the woods and Becky had helped her to rescue them.

"Hello, kitties!" called Katie, pushing open the mudroom door.

Immediately, Pixie, the silver-gray cat, stopped attacking the laces of the king's walking boots and pranced over. He weaved around Katie's legs, rubbing his head against her.

Katie scratched him under the chin. Pixie purred ecstatically, then suddenly a black-and-white ball of fluff cannoned into him, knocking him over.

"Bella, you are such a naughty kitten!" Katie exclaimed.

Pixie sprang up and cuffed Bella with a paw. Bella batted him back, and the two kittens rolled together on the floor.

"It's a good thing we don't play like that." Becky giggled.

"Can you imagine what Dad would say?" Katie agreed. She made her voice go deep like the king's. "Princesses *never* fight."

Becky dug into her pocket and pulled out a felt mouse with a long string tail. The mouse jingled as Becky showed it to Katie.

"Look what Mom bought for the kittens. It's got a bell inside and it smells like catnip, which cats love."

Becky put the mouse on the floor and pulled its long string. The mouse wiggled toward her. It looked so real that for a second Katie thought it had moved by itself. Immediately, Bella and Pixie stopped fighting and stared at the tinkling mouse. Then Bella pounced. But Becky was too quick, pulling the mouse just out of her reach.

"Look at her little face!" Katie couldn't stop laughing. Bella was so surprised. She crouched down, ears pricked, whiskers twitching. Her fluffy black tail stretched out behind her as she bunched her body and sprang at the mouse again.

"Missed!" Becky chuckled, pulling it out of her reach.

Soon it wasn't just Bella chasing the toy mouse. Pixie and Poppy joined in, too. Sometimes Becky let one of the kittens catch it, but not too often. It was more fun watching them skitter around after it.

"This is fun," said Katie when it was her turn to work the mouse. She lifted it off the ground, making the kittens jump in the air for it.

Katie was enjoying herself so much that she totally forgot about the time. It wasn't until the queen poked her head around the door that she remembered she had a dress fitting. It was Mom's birthday soon, and the king was holding a special birthday ball to celebrate. Katie was going to perform a dance for the queen in front of all the guests, and she was having a special dress made for the occasion. Her heart missed a beat. Would Mom be mad at her?

"Sorry, Mom," she said, handing the mouse to Becky and leaping to her feet.

The queen smiled. "It's all right, darling. You're not late yet. Have you seen Alfie? He's getting a new suit."

Alfie was Katie's little brother. He was sometimes annoying, but he looked up to his big sister and they mostly got along.

"Why is Alfie getting a new suit?" asked Katie. "I thought he was too young to go to the ball."

"He is, but your father has agreed that he can come and see you dance."

"Oh!" Katie's stomach fluttered nervously. She hoped Alfie would behave himself and not distract her!

Becky tucked the mouse back in her jeans pocket.

"I'd better go. Mom's been busy getting things ready for the ball, and I promised her I'd help with dinner tonight."

Mrs. Philips was the housekeeper at Starlight Palace, and Becky's family lived in

an apartment in the palace's west tower.

Katie and Becky said good-bye to the kittens. Bella grabbed ahold of Katie's jeans and wouldn't let go.

"Sorry, Bella, but I don't have time to play anymore."

Katie needed Becky's help to gently pull Bella away from her leg. Bella chased the girls to the door, so Katie opened it a crack and let Becky squeeze out first, then followed her. As the door shut, Bella cried in disappointment.

"I'll be back soon, kitties!" called Katie.

"Good luck with the dress fitting," said Becky.

"Thanks," said Katie, thinking she'd need it. She loved getting new dresses, but she wasn't excited about having them specially made. It meant standing still forever.

"See you tomorrow?" Katie asked.

"Definitely," said Becky.

Bella, the black-and-white kitten, stared at the door in disbelief. Why had Katie and Becky left so suddenly? Weren't they having fun together with the delicious-smelling jingly mouse? Feeling disappointed and let down, she sat on her bottom, lifted one black leg, and washed her white tummy. Next she cleaned her four white paws before starting on the rest of her body, finishing with her face. Daintily licking a paw, Bella wiped clean the white blaze down her nose, around

her head and green eyes, and finally her coal-black ears.

That felt better! And what's more, now Bella had a plan. She would go and find the girls and see if they'd let her play with the jingly mouse again. But how was she going to get out? Katie had pulled on the handle halfway up, but that was much too high for Bella to reach. As she stood wondering what to do next, the door opened and Alfie looked in.

"Katie? Oh, she must have gone to the fitting without me." He rushed off down the hall.

In his hurry, Alfie didn't shut the door all the way.

Barely able to believe her good luck, Bella slipped through it, then hesitated, not

sure which way to go. She sniffed the carpet.
To her left it was heavy with old scents, but
to her right it smelled flowery, like Katie.

"This way," Bella said to herself, pleased
with her cleverness.

Confidently, she set out down the hall to
find her friend.

Chapter 2

Ghost!

"Princess Katie, you can move now," said Mrs. Snippet, waving a handful of pins.

Katie let her breath out in a noisy whoosh of relief.

"I was scared you would prick me," she said.

Mrs. Snippet put the extra pins in a drawer

in her sewing box and smiled at Katie.

"I've been dressmaking for fifty years and haven't pricked anyone yet. But I suppose there's always a first time, Princess."

Katie grinned. "Well, I hope it won't be with me. Is my dress almost finished?"

"Almost. It's a little loose, so it needs to be taken in, and then there's the hem to do."

Mrs. Snippet pulled a measuring tape out of her pocket and slipped it around Katie's waist.

"Please don't make it too tight," said Katie, worried that she might not be able to dance in it.

"Don't worry. You can try it on again when I've finished," Mrs. Snippet reassured her.

Katie relaxed and stole a look in the full-length mirror. Her dress was the prettiest one she'd ever owned. It was purple, her favorite color, with a scooped neck and tiny sleeves. It went in at the waist and had two skirts, a purple one on top with a zigzag hem that showed off the sparkly pink skirt underneath. The dress was fastened at the back with a line of purple and pink rose-shaped buttons and had a matching rose at her waist. Katie was going to fin- ish it off with sparkly tights and sil- ver dance shoes.

There was a knock at the door. "Are you dressed?" called the queen.

"Yes, come on in," Katie answered.

Alfie bounded into the room first. "Wow!" he said, his eyes popping. "Is that a real rose?"

"Don't touch it," said Katie, stepping back.

"Are your hands clean?"

"Of course!" Alfie lunged for the rose at Katie's waist.

"Alfie! That's enough," said the queen sternly. "Go and sit on that stool until it's your turn."

Sticking his tongue out at Katie, Alfie sat on the stool.

Katie turned her back on him. "How should I wear my hair?" she asked. "Up or down?"

The queen tilted her head to one side as Katie twisted her long blond hair up into a bun.

"It looks lovely like that. Wear it up for the ball, and I'll lend you my tiara. It'll help keep your hair in place when you're dancing."

"Really?"

The tiara had been made for the queen to wear on her wedding day and was very special. Katie rushed forward and hugged her.

"Thank you. That'd be perfect!"

"Careful, Princess," said Mrs. Snippet.

"The dress is still pinned. You can take it off now. Go through to the sewing room, and I'll come and help you when I've written down these measurements."

Katie went into the room next door. Mrs. Snippet's sewing machine was on the table along with another sewing box stuffed full of needles, pins, scissors, and spools of thread. There were several dressmaker's dummies modeling the outfits that Mrs. Snippet was making for the ball.

Katie saw Alfie's small green velvet suit, her dad's gray one, her mother's dress, and an empty dummy that was for Katie's dress. The dummies didn't have heads and they made Katie giggle. There was something a little spooky about them, especially the one wearing her mom's long ball gown. Mrs. Snippet had covered the dress with a large white sheet so that the king didn't see it, since the queen wanted it to be a surprise. It made the dummy look like a ghost.

"There's no such thing as ghosts," Katie said sensibly to herself.

She started to undo the buttons on her dress. Then suddenly she heard a rustle.

What was that? Katie stared at the dummies. The sheet covering her mom's dress was twitching. An icy shiver ran up her spine.

No, she must have been imagining things. Katie blinked and looked again. This time, the sheet billowed just like a ghost.

"Aaargh!" Katie wanted to run away, but her feet seemed glued to the floor.

The sheet rose and fell again. Katie's heart was thudding so hard it hurt. Forcing her legs to work, she started to back away. Something small and black-and-white shot out from under the sheet, then disappeared. Katie stared in disbelief as a pink nose appeared next.

"Oh, no!" she groaned.

Walking forward, she carefully lifted the sheet.

"Bella! What are you doing here?"

"Meow!" Bella stared at Katie with big green eyes, then stalked into the open.

"Aaargghh!" shrieked Mrs. Snippet, who had chosen that moment to come in. "A cat! Shoo!" she added, flapping her hands. "Shoo, shoo."

"It's all right, Mrs. Snippet. I'll get her," said Katie.

"Princess, stop! Think of the cat hairs. And claws! You'll snag your new dress."

Mrs. Snippet tutted crossly as she ushered Bella to the door.

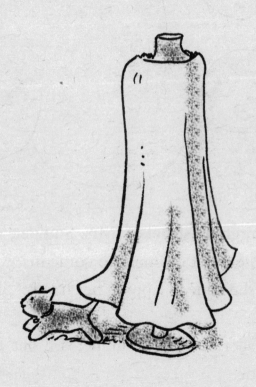

Bella looked confused. Katie wanted to pick her up, but she didn't dare.

"It's okay, Bella," she called as Mrs. Snippet guided the kitten back to the hall, then shut the door on her.

"It's *not* okay!" huffed Mrs. Snippet. "I *never* want to see that kitten here again. If anything happens to your new dress, what will you wear to the ball?"

"Sorry," said Katie meekly. "I promise I'll make sure Bella stays away."

The moment Katie was back in her jeans and T-shirt, she raced out of the sewing room to find Bella. The little black-and-white kitten was waiting sadly outside the door. She meowed loudly when she saw Katie.

"Oh, Bella!" said Katie, scooping her up

and pressing her cheek against Bella's silky fur. "You have to stay out of Mrs. Snippet's room."

On the way to the mudroom, Katie bumped into the king.

"Hello, darling. How's my favorite princess today?" he asked.

"I'm fine, thanks, Dad," said Katie.

"And how's your dance coming along for the birthday ball?"

"Well, it's okay."

"I hope it's better than okay!" The king smiled. "I've promised the queen she's going to have the best birthday ball ever."

Katie grinned. "You say that every year."

"But this year is *extra* special," said the king. "Your mother's been working very hard, and she deserves a treat. Promise you won't let me down?"

"I promise."

"That's my girl." The king patted Katie's arm before going on his way.

Anxiously, Katie carried the wriggling

Bella to the mudroom. The kitten was so curious. Katie hoped she could keep her out of trouble. It would be a disaster if Bella's playful ways ruined Mom's birthday ball.

Chapter 3

Something Fishy

Bella loved to play. Along with the jingly mouse that smelled so good, the girls brought other toys. The scratching post was so much fun. Bella loved running her claws down it. At the top of the post was a platform to sit on, which she hadn't managed to climb up to yet, but she had fun trying. When she grew too frustrated, she batted at the ball hanging from the platform.

The tunnel was another favorite. It was dark inside and rustled when she walked through it. It was also a good place to hide. Bella had invented a game where she hid in the tunnel and pounced on the other kittens when they walked past.

But Bella's favorite games were the ones when Katie and Becky joined in. The girls were so much fun, teasing her with the jingly mouse and rolling balls for her to chase. They brought cat treats with them, too. The fishy ones were delicious!

One morning, Katie came alone.

"Becky went shopping with her mom to buy a dress for the ball," she explained.

Bella didn't understand and was disappointed when Katie didn't stay long with her. She'd been hoping for a game of chase the mouse! But after feeding the kittens and giving them fresh water, Katie left, saying, "I'll come and play with you this afternoon. I'm riding Misty now, and then I have an extra dance lesson."

Bella wandered over to Pixie, who was sunning himself by the window.

"Come and play with me," she mewed.

Pixie yawned. "Later, when I'm not so full of breakfast."

Tortoiseshell Poppy was washing up. One leg was in the air as she cleaned her tummy.

"Come and play," said Bella, pouncing on her tail.

"I'm busy," purred Poppy.

The other kittens were curled up together in the basket. None of them wanted to play

with Bella, either. Halfheartedly, Bella batted a ball around. She hit the ball harder and harder until it rolled into the wall and

bounced back at her. That was fun! Bella kept hitting the ball to see how far she could bounce it off the wall.

"Ouch!" squeaked Poppy loudly as the ball accidently hit her on the nose.

"Sorry," said Bella, running after it.

The ball landed in the basket and Bella dived in to get it.

"Get off!" squealed Tilly.

"Bella," yowled the rest of the kittens, batting at her with their paws.

Bella hooked the ball out of the basket. She rolled it across the floor and skittered after it. The ball pinged off the scratching post and into the mouth of the tunnel. The tunnel rustled noisily as Bella chased the ball and knocked it out the other end. Now where had it gone? Bella jumped out of the tunnel in time to see the ball rolling across the room. Chasing after it, she swished it with a paw. The ball spun across the room, bounced off a shoe, and landed in the water bowl, splashing Pixie.

"Bella!" he growled, his whiskers twitching angrily. "Go and play somewhere else."

The ball bobbed in the water bowl. Bella hesitated. She didn't like getting her paws wet. Reluctantly, she left the ball where it was and went to sit by the door, fixing it with her bright green eyes as if staring at it would make it open. She sat there for a long time, until at last her efforts were rewarded. Slowly, the door swung wide.

Bella jumped up, but as she tried to go through the gap, a hand pushed her gently back.

"No, little one. I'm not here to let you out. I'm here to clean the room."

"Please?" Bella pleaded.

"I know," said the maid, totally misunderstanding her cries. "I don't know how I'm supposed to clean with so many kittens in here, either."

Sighing heavily, the maid began lifting her cleaning equipment into the room. Bella waited until her back was turned, then

slipped into the hallway. This time Bella didn't stop to work out which way Katie had gone. She scampered off before the maid could notice her escaping.

After a while, the carpet ended and large tiles covered the floor. Bella didn't like the tiles. Her paws slipped on them and she had to slow down.

There were lots of doors. Most of them were shut, and Bella wondered what was inside the rooms. Then a delicious smell wafted toward her. Bella's nose twitched and her stomach grumbled hungrily. Breakfast had been a long time ago. Eagerly, she followed the lovely smell.

Her search took her to a room at the end of the hall. There was a lot of noise coming from it, but the smell was so wonderful, Bella forgot to be scared. She slipped inside and found the room full of people dressed in white hats and large aprons. It was very hot and everyone was red in the face. Bella's paws twitched with excitement. There was so much food here. A pair of legs strode toward her. Quickly, Bella hid under a table. As she watched the activity, she smelled something particularly delicious.

Fish.

Bella swished her tail. Half closing her eyes, she worked out that the fish was on the counter where a lady was working. The lady had a kind face and Bella was about to ask her for a scrap of fish when the lady was called away.

"Whiskers!" Now she would have to wait.

Bella curled her black tail neatly around
her white paws and stared at the counter.
She waited for ages. At last she couldn't bear
it any longer. Silently, she crept from under
the table. The counter was too high to reach,

but there was a box next to it. Stretching
up, she rested her front paws on the lid and
pulled herself on top. That was easy, but the
counter was still too high to reach.

Bella looked around. That nearby chair might work! Taking a deep breath, she bunched her body and sprang, landing on the seat. Bella dug her claws in to stop herself from sliding off. She reached up and put her front paws on the counter. It was hard and slippery, but the fishy smell was driving her crazy.

Slowly, Bella pulled herself up. Her nose

was level with the countertop when her paws began to slip. Bella stuck out her claws but it was no use—she couldn't get a good grip. In a rush of air, she fell. Instinctively, she twisted her body and somehow landed on her front paws. Then her bottom caught up, flipping her head over heels. Bella rolled across the floor until she bumped into a pair of shiny black shoes.

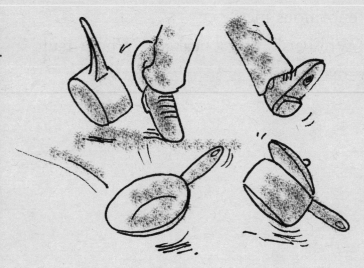

"What . . ." cried a man's voice.

There was a huge crash as he tripped over Bella. Several louder crashes and lots of angry voices quickly followed. Bella curled into a ball, keeping her eyes tightly shut. The banging and crashing was frightening. It went on for a long time but at last it stopped. Bella timidly uncurled and looked around. The shiny kitchen was now an enormous mess.

"Whiskers!" she squeaked. "Whose fault was that?"

Chapter 4

Bella in Trouble

Princess Katie threw open her bedroom door and pirouetted across the room. Her dance lesson had gone really well and Madame Quickstep was pleased with her. If she could dance like that at the birthday ball, Mom and Dad would be happy, too. Cheerfully, Katie danced into her dressing room and wriggled out of her dancing dress.

"What should I wear?" she said to herself.

Princess Katie had a lot of pretty clothes, but there was no point in dressing up when she was going to play with the kittens.

"I know," she said, picking up an old blue T-shirt with a picture of a horse on it. She put it on, along with faded jeans with daisies on the pockets.

Katie couldn't wait to play with the kittens, especially Bella, who was so much fun. Shoving her feet into a pair of sneakers, she went to see if Becky was back from shopping. The girls met downstairs.

"Did you get a dress?" asked Katie.

"Yes," said Becky, her brown eyes shining. "It's silver and blue."

"It sounds pretty." Katie had just opened the mudroom door when an enormous crash came from farther down the hallway. Silence followed, then there were more crashes and lots of shouting.

Katie's heart sank to her sneakers. She had a bad feeling about the noise. She quickly did a kitten count.

"Five," she said. "Who's missing?"

"Bella!" Katie and Becky spoke together.

Wordlessly, the girls followed the noise until they arrived at the kitchen. It was chaos! Saucepans and smashed plates littered the floor. There was a puddle of chocolate sauce and a trail of icing. A maid sat in the middle of it all with a lap full of squashed strawberries. Other kitchen staff members were running around, bumping into one another and making more mess as they chased after a small fluffy kitten.

"Oh, Bella!" gasped Katie.

Bella's black-and-white fur stood upright, and her tail was as straight and stiff as a broomstick. Her green eyes were wide with terror as she darted around the room. One of the cooks almost caught her, but Bella changed direction and collided with a chef who was putting a huge cake into a cupboard, out of harm's way.

The chef lost his balance. Holding tightly to the cake, he tried to right himself. Then a maid slipped in the chocolate sauce and crashed into him.

"Help!" shouted the chef, toppling forward. Katie felt like she was watching everything in slow motion. The chef raised his hands, which were holding the cake, but as he hit the ground he dropped it. The cake flew through the air.

"Quick!" Becky dashed forward.

Katie snapped into action but neither of the girls was fast enough. The cake hit the

floor and exploded. Cake and icing flew in all directions and a splotch of jam landed on the chef's head.

Katie's chest felt so tight she could hardly breathe. The cake was ruined. Something nudged at her leg. Katie looked down and saw that it was Bella, leaning against her as she cleaned icing from her whiskers.

"Oh, Bella!" Bending down, Katie scooped the kitten into her arms. "We're in *big* trouble now."

Bella nuzzled her face against Katie's cheek. She was trembling and her ears were flat back.

"It's okay," said Katie softly. "You're safe here."

Katie and Becky petted her head. Bella began to relax and pushed her head against their hands.

The head cook came over. She was red in the face and she was shaking.

"Ruined!" she moaned. "It took days to make that cake. And look at the state of my beautiful kitchen!"

"I'm sorry," said Katie, blinking back tears. "We'll help clean it up, won't we, Becky?"

The cook shook her head. "The mess isn't the biggest problem. That was the queen's birthday cake! How are we going to replace it in time? Just go, Princess, and take that kitten with you."

What if the head cook couldn't make another cake? The ball would be ruined. Her mom would be so upset and Dad would be furious. Back in the mudroom, she sat down with Bella in her lap.

"Listen, Bella, Dad's going to be very angry when he finds out what you've done. You have got to behave or he might send you away."

Becky went white. "He wouldn't do that!"

"He might," said Katie sadly. "He wants Mom to have the best birthday ball ever."

"It's not Bella's fault. She has too much energy. We need to tire her out more," said Becky. "If we play lots of exciting games with her, then she'll sleep more and not get into so much trouble."

"That's a great idea," said Katie.

Katie looked at the collection of cat toys thoughtfully.

"Let's build an obstacle course. She'd love it and it would tire her out! But first I have to go see Dad. If I tell him what happened and how we're going to keep Bella busy, he might not be so mad."

"I'll come with you," Becky offered.

"Thanks," said Katie gratefully, "but this is something I have to do on my own."

The king was furious. At first, he wanted to give Bella away.

"Look at all the trouble she's caused. Everyone's working so hard. It's not fair to have their efforts ruined by a bad kitten."

Katie clenched her hands together. Swallowing back the tears, she said, "Please, Dad, give her another chance."

The king sighed. "One more chance," he said at last.

"Thank you!" Katie flung her arms around his neck.

Promising to keep an extra special eye on

Bella in future, she ran back to the mudroom to tell Becky the good news.

"Phew!" said Becky. "Let's start tiring Bella out, then."

Bella and the other kittens watched curiously while Katie and Becky put together an obstacle course. It started with a tunnel for Bella to crawl through. At the end of the tunnel, she had to chase the jingly mouse.

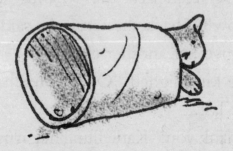

"Next we'll lead her over to the scratching post," said Becky.

Katie found an old
shoe box and put it by
the scratching post so
that Bella could
reach the platform. She
placed a fishy cat treat

on the top to tempt the kitten up there,
and Becky put a cushion on the other side
for her to jump down onto. Next Bella
would bat the ball over to another tunnel
made by pushing two chairs together.

"And we'll finish by getting her to weave
between all the rain boots," said Katie. She
arranged the collection of boots in a long
line, putting cat treats between them to
show Bella the way.

"It looks like fun," said Becky. "I'd love to
try it out."

"You're too big for the cat tunnel. And I'd like to see you sitting on top of the scratching post!" Katie giggled.

Katie picked up Bella and put her at the start of the course. At first she tried to eat the cat treats without going around the obstacles.

Katie and Becky patiently took her back

to the beginning of the tunnel until finally she got the hang of it. Pixie wanted a turn, too. Then Poppy hid under the chairs and pounced on Bella as she crawled under them. The two kittens rolled around until Pixie jumped on them both. Soon all six kittens were play fighting, chasing one another around the obstacle course and the room. Katie and Becky couldn't stop laughing.

"Did you see that?" Katie chuckled. She was laughing so hard she could hardly speak. "Pixie was sitting on top of the scratching post batting everyone below, and then he fell off."

"Poppy was funny, too," giggled Becky. "She batted the ball and accidentally flipped it over her head. She almost fell over trying to see where it had gone."

After a while the kittens began to get tired. One by one, they flopped down in their basket. Bella was the last to stop playing. Sleepily, she climbed in the basket, squeezing between Pixie and Poppy.

"It worked!" said Becky.

"Yes," said Katie. "There's just one problem."

"What is it?"

"The mess!" said Katie, eyeing the room.

While she and Becky were cleaning up, Katie wondered how things were going in the kitchen. The cook was very good at producing food on short notice, but the queen's birthday ball was in three days. Could she bake and ice a new birthday cake by then?

Chapter 5

Fun in the Barn

Early the next day, Princess Katie and Becky took the kittens down to the barn to play, carrying the kittens in a large cardboard box.

The kittens didn't like being shut in. They mewed loudly and wriggled around and it was awkward to hold them. At the entrance to the maze, Katie and Becky stopped for a break, sitting on a bench with the box between them. A peacock strutted over, neck stretched, his head to one side. His magnificent tail was closed and it brushed along the ground. Curiously, he eyed the box.

"If you show us your lovely tail, we'll show you what's in the box," joked Becky.

The peacock fixed Becky with a steely eye.

"He doesn't like that idea," said Katie with a giggle.

A scuffling noise caught her attention. A

white paw poked between the flaps of the cardboard box.

"Bella!" squeaked Katie. "You're too good at escaping!"

Reaching into the box, she lifted Bella out and held her up to the peacock. The animals stared at each other for a second, then Bella hissed. The peacock drew back and stalked away.

"That wasn't very nice," scolded Katie.

Bella stiffened, then suddenly tried to wriggle free.

"Oh, no you don't!" said Katie, following her gaze to a squirrel at the base of a tree.

Hurriedly, she put Bella back in the box, saying, "You can play when we get to the barn."

Bella hated riding in the box. She didn't mind the dark, but she didn't like not being able to see where she was going. The minute Katie opened the lid, she jumped out. Then, remembering what Mom had told her a long time ago, she looked around, checking out her surroundings.

"Purrip," squeaked Bella, recognizing the barn. This was a safe place.

Whiskers twitching, she stalked around, taking in all the exciting smells.

Katie and Becky got busy dragging hay bales around. Bella went over to see what they were doing.

"Out of the way, Bella," said Katie, gently moving her.

Katie had soft hands and a kind voice. But best of all she knew just where Bella liked to be scratched. Bella nudged Katie with her head, purring ecstatically when Katie rubbed

her under the
chin. Each time
Katie stopped
scratching,
Bella butted
her hand.

"You're
funny," Katie
giggled, sitting
her on a hay
bale.

It didn't take long for Bella to guess what
Katie and Becky were doing. They were
building her another obstacle course! She
could hardly wait and wanted to help, but
every time she tried, someone picked her
up and put her back on the hay bale. Bella's
tail twitched with frustration until, at last,

the course was finished. Katie carried her to the start, then Becky showed her which way to go by waving a long stick with ribbons attached.

Bella couldn't decide which was more fun—chasing the ribbons or scrambling over the obstacle course. Her brothers and sisters loved it all, too. Pebbles turned it into a race. He and Bella ran around, scrambling

over hay bales and crawling through the tunnels. When the kittens began to get tired, Bella started a game of hide-and-seek. She was very good at hiding, jumping on the other kittens when they least expected it.

Long after the other kittens had collapsed in a heap, Bella was still playing. She was disappointed when Katie began to dismantle the obstacle course and put the kittens back in their box.

At last, Katie picked up Bella and hugged

her. Bella loved being held. Princess Katie
was soft and warm and she could hear her
heart thumping. Bella stared at Katie, her
green eyes wide and pleading.

"Play with me," she purred.

But Katie lowered her into the box,

holding her tighter when she tried to wriggle free. It made Bella mad to be back in the dark with the others.

"Why can't we stay here?" she complained when the box began to move.

"We don't live here. Our basket is in the mudroom," said Pixie reasonably.

"Stupid mudroom," grumbled Bella. Starlight Palace was such an amazing place, she wanted to be allowed to go wherever she liked. Well, she wouldn't stay put. She was getting good at finding ways out. Settling down in the box, Bella began to plot her next adventure.

It turned out to be much easier than Bella could have hoped. Not long after Katie and Becky returned the kittens to the mud-room, firmly closing the door behind them, Alfie came in.

"I'm bored!" he sighed. "Everyone's too busy with the silly birthday ball to play with me. But you'll play with me, won't you?"

Alfie picked up the jingly mouse and waved it under Bella's nose. At once she pounced, giving chase as Alfie ran across the room. It was a lot of fun and Bella was very disappointed when the queen came to tell Alfie he was late for his music lesson.

"See you soon!" Alfie called to the kit-

tens, rushing out and forgetting to close the door again.

"Who wants to explore?" Bella called to her brothers and sisters.

"Me!" squeaked everyone.

Bella's paws tingled with excitement as the other five kittens joined her outside the room.

"Which way?" asked Poppy.

Bella stared around. The kitchen was that way. As delicious as it smelled, she wasn't

sure she wanted to go there again. It had been too scary.

"This way!" she said, setting out in the opposite direction.

Chapter 6

Missing Again!

"Stop!" called Madame Quickstep, clapping her hands together.

Katie landed awkwardly, flinging out her arms to balance herself.

"Do that again, from the glissade. And stop holding your head as if you're carrying china on it!" scolded Madame Quickstep.

"The tiara is *not* going to fall off."

Katie bit back a scowl. It was all very well for Madame Quickstep to be upset, but Katie had never worn the queen's tiara before, and it felt weird. It was silver, with three points that each had a silver star on top. There was a huge purple amethyst in the middle, and

pink and white diamonds studded around the sides. It was much bigger and heavier than the tiara she normally danced in, and she kept thinking it was going to slide over her nose.

Forcing herself to smile politely, Katie nodded at the pianist to show she was ready, then set off across the floor. She desperately wanted to touch the tiara to check that it was still in place, but instead she kept her hands where they should be, letting her feet carry her to the final part of the dance. This was the tricky part—*run, leap, and fly.* Katie landed with her feet neatly together, twirled a pirouette, and finished with her hands in the air.

"Bravo!" cheered Madame Quickstep. "That was excellent. Tomorrow, come to my lesson wearing your new dress and silver shoes. You'd better practice dancing in them, too."

"I will. See you tomorrow, Madame!"
Pulling the tiara off, Katie smiled with relief.

"I'll go and ask Mrs. Snippet if my dress
is ready," she said to herself when she had
changed out of her dancing clothes.

She went to the sewing room and knocked
on the door.

"Come in," called Mrs. Snippet. "Hello,
Princess, this is a nice surprise."

"Hello," said Katie, stepping into the room. "Is that Mom's dress you're working on?"

"Yes. I'm almost done. I've been sewing lace around the hem. It's taken me a long time. What do you think?"

Mrs. Snippet held up the skirt of the queen's dress for Katie to see.

"Oh," said Katie, smiling to cover her dismay.

The lace was nice but a little old-fashioned. The dress looked prettier without it. "I . . . It . . . I think it's lovely," she said bravely.

"Me too," sighed Mrs. Snippet. "It's the perfect finishing touch."

"I wondered if my dress was done?" asked Katie, quickly changing the subject. "Madame Quickstep wants me to practice dancing in it."

"Sorry, Princess, but I've been working on this all day. I'll start on your dress first thing tomorrow."

"Thank you." Swallowing her disappointment, Katie left Mrs. Snippet to her work. Tomorrow was her last dance lesson, and the queen's birthday ball was the day after. Trying not to worry that she would have no time to practice dancing in her dress, Katie went to give the kittens their dinner. She was surprised to find the mudroom door open. Her heart sank as she entered the room. It was empty. The kittens had escaped!

"No," she groaned, covering her face with her hands.

Dashing into the hallway, Katie ran headfirst into Alfie.

"Hi," he said cheerfully. "I've come to see the kittens again."

Katie's eyes narrowed suspiciously. *"Again?"*

"Yes," said Alfie.

"Alfie! You left the door open, and the kittens escaped."

"I didn't," he argued.

"You must have."

Alfie stamped his foot. "Didn't."

"What's going on?" asked Becky as she walked in. "Why are you arguing?"

"The kittens escaped," said Katie. Turning to Alfie, she added, "*Someone* forgot to shut the door!"

"We'd better find them before they get into trouble," said Becky sensibly. "You go this way, Katie. Alfie, you go that way, and I'll look in the kitchens."

Katie felt suddenly sick. What if Bella was in the kitchens again? There wasn't time to start on yet another birthday cake. The ball would be ruined, and Bella would definitely be sent away.

"I've got a better idea," said Alfie suddenly.

"It's nearly dinnertime isn't it? Wait here a minute."

He ran off and returned carrying a metal feeding bowl and a fork. "Watch this," he said.

Banging the fork against the bowl, he yelled, "Here, kitties, time for dinner!"

Katie and Becky jumped in surprise and covered their ears with their hands as Alfie continued to beat on the bowl.

Sure enough, a few seconds later, Pixie appeared with Poppy trotting after him.

"Wow! That was so smart, Alfie," said Katie, impressed with his quick thinking.

Katie and Becky ushered the kittens into the mudroom. Pebbles and Tilly came next, and a few minutes later the white kitten, Suki. She raced toward them and almost fell head over heels as she skidded into the mudroom.

"Careful!" said Katie, bending down to catch her.

"Three . . . four . . . five," counted Becky. "So who's missing?"

"Bella!" chorused everyone.

Alfie kept banging the food bowl, but either Bella couldn't hear it or she was choosing to ignore it.

"Alfie, can you feed the kittens while we go and find Bella? They get a third of a can of kitten food each. You have to watch to make sure they don't eat each other's food, and they need fresh water," Katie told him.

Alfie went pink with pleasure. "Of course I can do it!" he said.

Katie's heart banged loudly as she and Becky started their search. Where had Bella gone *this* time?

Bella was having fun. Starlight Palace was enormous, with lots of different and exciting rooms to explore. She rolled on thick carpets, played pouncing games with patches of sunlight, hid under chairs, and climbed up some curtains. The curtains had a lovely velvety feel, but when she was halfway up, 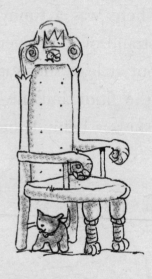 they began to swing. Alarmed, Bella dug her claws in harder. Gradually, the curtains slowed until Bella decided it was safe to get down. But now one of her claws was stuck.

She tried to pull herself free, but that made the curtain sway faster again. Bella's fur fluffed out in alarm. Desperate to get back to the ground, she yanked her paw away as hard as she could. There was a funny ripping sound. A small strand of red velvet was stuck in her claw, but at least she was free. She scrambled to the floor and nibbled the velvet free as she sat behind the curtain.

Ready to go exploring again, Bella left
the room and found a staircase that twirled
upward. It was fun to climb and led to even
more exciting rooms, one full of toys. There
were cuddly animals and a wooden castle
and a train set, but Bella loved the car the
best. It was big enough for her to sit on, and,
by running at the car and jumping on top
of it, Bella got a ride. Soon she'd invented a
new game, seeing how far she could get the

car to zoom across the floor.

A long time later, Bella had finally had enough of playing with the toys. She was tired, her paws ached, and she longed for her friends. She padded along the hallway looking for Katie, Becky, or her new friend Alfie. Bella nosed open a door. Was Katie in here? Bella hoped so. The room looked familiar—it was the one with the dummies dressed up in clothes. Katie had been here once, so maybe she'd come again.

Bella crawled hopefully under the long white sheet to wait for her. Underneath the sheet, she was surprised to find the silky dress now had some pretty lacy stuff at the bottom. Bella kneaded the material with her paws. It felt wonderful! When she was comfortable, she settled down with her face pressed against it. Sleepily, she closed her eyes. She half heard someone enter the room and a little while later the click of a door, but she was too tired to go and investigate.

Much later, Bella woke up. Yawning lazily, she stretched out her paws. Her tummy growled emptily—it must be dinnertime. Bella stood up, but the lacy fabric stuck to her claws.

Each time she yanked a paw free, there was a funny ripping sound. It reminded Bella of the velvet curtains, only the ripping lace felt much nicer. Bella rolled around, fighting the lace, loving the sound and feel of it as it tore, until her stomach growled again. Remembering it was dinnertime, she finally

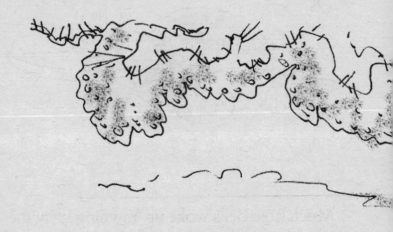

freed her claws and nosed her way from under the dress and sheet. The room was in semidarkness, but Bella could see well and made her way to the door.

To her dismay, it was shut. Bella scratched it with her claws. That didn't help. She jumped for the door handle, but it

was too high for her to reach. Desperate to get out, Bella kept clawing at the door. But it was no use. Bella's heart thudded uncomfortably as she realized she was trapped.

Chapter 7

Ruined!

"Where's Bella?" asked Katie for the umpteenth time.

The queen perched on the edge of Katie's bed. "She'll be in the palace somewhere," she said reassuringly.

"But what if she's causing trouble?" wailed Katie.

"Bella will be fine," said the queen, smoothing Katie's comforter. "You tired her out today, so I'm sure she's curled up somewhere fast asleep. Stop worrying and get some rest. You've got a busy couple of days coming up."

Katie sighed as she settled down. But long after Mom had hugged her good night, she

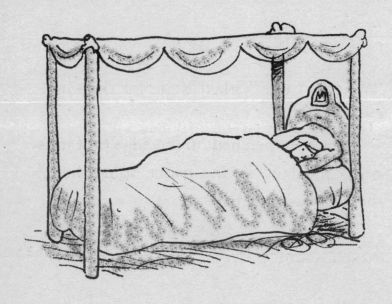

was still wide awake and worrying about Bella. The nights were still very cold. What if the kitten had strayed outside? Or worse yet, what if she wasn't tired and was causing trouble somewhere? According to Becky, the new birthday cake had been made and was waiting to be iced. What if Bella got into the kitchen and wrecked it?

Katie drifted into a restless sleep and woke up very early the next morning. Unable to stay in bed, she got up and immediately went to look for Bella. She started at the mudroom in case the little kitten had somehow found her way back there. Instead she found Becky, peering at the five sleeping kittens.

"What are you doing here?" asked Katie in surprise.

"Same as you," Becky sighed. "I couldn't sleep last night because I was worrying about Bella. I even got Mom to go and check the kitchens for me, but luckily Bella wasn't there."

Quietly, the girls searched the palace. They weren't the only ones up so early. There were a lot of people hard at work preparing for the queen's birthday ball, putting up sparkling decorations, arranging wonderfully scented flowers, practicing music, and stringing up lights. Katie and Becky kept out of their way as they searched the ground floor, then took the elevator to the second. As the elevator doors slid open, there was a shrill scream. Katie went ice cold. She recognized that voice. Fearfully, she and Becky ran to the sewing room, where Mrs. Snippet was in a flood of tears.

"What's wrong?" asked Katie, giving her a hug.

"It's ruined!" sobbed the dressmaker. "The queen's dress is ruined. Th-th-that naughty kitten ripped all the lace."

Katie's chest was so tight she could hardly breathe as Mrs. Snippet held out the ruined dress. From the corner of her eye she could see Bella cowering in the corner. Katie's relief at finding the kitten was replaced with a sick fear. If Mom's dress was ruined, then so was the birthday ball!

"Torn and covered in cat hair," moaned Mrs. Snippet, putting her face in her hands.

"Can I take a look?" asked Becky. Stepping forward, she took a long look at the dress.

"It's not as bad as you think," she said at last. "Mom has a special clothes brush that will get rid of the cat hair. And it's only the lace hem  that's torn. Not the dress. If you took it off really carefully, I don't think anyone would know."

Katie felt a tiny spark of hope. "The dress did look pretty even without the lace," she said.

Mrs. Snippet dried her eyes. While she examined the dress, Katie picked Bella up. She was trembling with fright and Katie petted the kitten's head to calm her down.

As Bella relaxed, she snuggled into Katie's chest.

"Oh, Bella, you've really done it this time," whispered Katie sadly. If Mrs. Snippet couldn't fix Mom's dress, Bella would have to go.

"Well," said Mrs. Snippet finally. "I'm not sure I can take the lace off without making holes in the material, but I'll try. It's going to take a long time to remake the hem, though, and I still have *your* dress to finish. Let's hope I get everything done in time."

Princess Katie was so worried about her mother's dress that she did badly at her last dance lesson. Madame Quickstep shook her head with disappointment.

"I'm very sorry, Princess, but after that performance, I don't think I can let you dance at the ball."

Katie gasped. "*Please* let me," she pleaded. "I won't go riding. I'll stay here and practice instead."

Madame Quickstep sighed. "Very well. But only if you promise to concentrate!"

Katie was sad to miss her riding lesson, but the dance was more important. By the end of the day, she was exhausted and close to tears, especially when she learned that

the queen's dress *still* wasn't finished. It was a much bigger job than Mrs. Snippet had realized, and now she'd run out of thread.

She'd ordered more by special delivery, but the thread was coming from a long way away. Kind Mrs. Snippet offered to stay in the palace overnight so that she'd be ready to start work the moment the thread arrived.

Princess Katie had another night sleepless with worry. The birthday cake was finished, but what about the dresses? The following morning she was so tired it was a struggle to get out of bed. But there wasn't time

to sleep in. It was Mom's birthday and tonight there would be a ball in her honor. If she had a dress! Shoving her arms into her robe, Katie ran along to Mrs. Snippet's room to see if the thread had arrived.

Chapter 8

Clever Alfie

Princess Katie stood in the middle of the packed ballroom, feet together, head up. It was so quiet you could have heard a mouse squeak. Nervously, she looked around at the sea of people waiting for her to dance. They were wearing the most amazing clothes and jewelry.

But the queen looked the most beautiful, dressed in her blue ball gown, stitched with tiny silk flowers from the shoulder to the hem. Mrs. Snippet had done an amazing job. No one would ever guess that the dress had been damaged.

Katie was very conscious of her own ball gown. There hadn't been time to practice in it. It felt stiff and unfamiliar. Would she be able to dance in it? After everything that had happened, it would be awful if she ruined the ball by dancing badly. Her heart fluttered wildly until she remembered Madame Quickstep's advice.

Don't think about the dress. Take deep breaths and concentrate on the dance.

Katie breathed in deeply and started to feel

better. She nodded to the pianist, counting herself in as the music started. Slowly, she raised her arms, took three steps forward, turned, and jumped. The dress caught around her legs and she wobbled slightly. Gathering herself together, she danced across the floor,

but now she was on the wrong leg for the next jump.

Concentrate! she scolded herself.

As Katie came out of the jump, she almost fell over with surprise. What was Alfie doing under that table? Her eyes wanted to follow him, but she forced

herself to ignore her little brother. As she turned again, she caught another glimpse of him. He had one hand clutched to his chest as he slowly crawled along. Katie blinked and forced the picture out of her mind. She was determined not to let Alfie ruin her dance. She was getting used to the feel of her dress, but the tricky part was still to come.

Katie's silver shoes sparkled as she leaped into the air, her purple and pink skirts billowing as she finished with a pirouette. Hands above her head, she held the pose, then slowly curtsied to her audience.

The room fell silent. Katie looked for Mom. There she was, right at the front, looking beau-tiful and smiling proudly. The queen blew her a kiss and Katie blew one back.

"Bravo," called the king, clapping loudly. The guests clapped, too, cheering and calling for an encore. Katie was relieved when Madame Quickstep appeared by her side to lead her off. She'd really enjoyed dancing, but she couldn't face doing it all over again.

Katie hardly heard Madame Quickstep telling her how well she'd performed. She was too upset with Alfie.

Dad patted her arm, then Mom hugged her, saying, "Thank you, darling! That was wonderful. This is my *best* birthday ball ever!"

Katie forced a smile. It was a good thing they hadn't seen Alfie. What was he up to?

She had to find out before he ruined the evening.

The king and queen returned to their guests and Katie found Becky and told her what she'd seen.

"Ball gowns weren't meant for running in," said Becky, holding up her silver-and blue-skirt as she hurried from the ballroom.

"You should try dancing in one!" Katie exclaimed.

The long hallway outside was empty.

"Where's Alfie?" said Becky, staring up and down the hall.

"He's *such* a pain. He's almost as bad as Bella sometimes," sighed Katie.

Suddenly, Katie and Becky stared at each other.

"Bella!" they exclaimed.

"*No!*" gasped Becky, her eyes wide. "She wouldn't . . ."

"It would be just like her," said Katie.

Together they tore down the hall to the mudroom. There was a lot of noise coming from inside. Katie opened the door and found Alfie rolling on the floor in his new green velvet suit, teasing Bella with the jingly mouse. He sat up guiltily.

"Sorry, Katie, I missed your dance. I

heard the clapping, though, so it must have been good."

"*I* saw *you*, though," said Katie. "You were under a table!"

Alfie turned bright red. "Did anyone else see me?"

"No," said Becky, a smile creeping to her

lips. "It was Bella's fault wasn't it?"

Alfie nodded. "She escaped again. It was lucky I saw her. She was climbing up to the food table to get to the prawns!"

"So you caught her and brought her back here?" asked Katie.

Alfie nodded. "I really wanted to see your dance, but I thought I'd better play with Bella in case she tried to escape again."

"Oh, wow!" said Becky. "Alfie, you're a little brother in a million!"

Alfie turned even redder.

Katie blushed, too, guiltily remembering how she thought Alfie was getting in trouble. Thinking hard, she tapped the carpet with one silver foot.

"I love all my kittens," she said slowly, "but I don't have enough time to look after

Bella. She's the sort of cat that needs one owner to give her lots of attention. Alfie, would you like to have Bella? She can still live here with the other kittens, but I'm sure she wouldn't get into as much trouble if you were looking after her."

"Really?"

Alfie picked up Bella and hugged her to him. "Did you hear that, Bella? You're my cat now."

"Is that a yes?" asked Katie with a grin.

"Yes!" yelled Alfie. "Thank you, Katie, you're the best sister ever! And Bella's the best kitten. Are you sure you won't miss her?"

Katie looked at the other five kittens squashed together in their basket.

"A little, but I'll still see her every day and the others will keep us busy, won't they, Becky?"

Becky smiled. "I think they will!"

Princess Katie's Kittens

Princess Katie's Kittens

Pixie at the Palace

Julie Sykes

SCHOLASTIC

Princess Katie's Kittens

Bella at the Ball

Julie Sykes

SCHOLASTIC

Princess
Katie's
Kittens

Collect all the kittens!

Pixie
at the Palace

One of the newly found kittens is missing
in the woods. Can Princess Katie and her
best friend, Becky, find Pixie and bring him
safely back to Starlight Palace?

WHERE EVERY PUPPY FINDS A HOME

PET HOTEL

Look who's checking in at the Pet Hotel!

PET HOTEL
Calling All Pets!

KATE FINCH · SCHOLASTIC

PET HOTEL
A Big Surprise

KATE FINCH · SCHOLASTIC

PET HOTEL
A Nose for Trouble

KATE FINCH · SCHOLASTIC

PET HOTEL
On with the Show!

KATE FINCH · SCHOLASTIC

Check out the exciting adventures of the Thea Sisters!

Thea Stilton and the Dragon's Code

Thea Stilton and the Mountain of Fire

Thea Stilton and the Ghost of the Shipwreck

Thea Stilton and the Secret City

Thea Stilton and the Mystery in Paris

Thea Stilton and the Cherry Blossom Adventure

Thea Stilton and the Star Castaways

Thea Stilton: Big Trouble in the Big Apple

Thea Stilton and the Ice Treasure

Thea Stilton and the Secret of the Old Castle

Thea Stilton and the Blue Scarab Hunt

Thea Stilton and the Prince's Emerald

Thea Stilton and the Mystery on the Orient Express

Thea Stilton and the Dancing Shadows

Thea Stilton and the Legend of the Fire Flowers

Thea Stilton and the Spanish Dance Mission

Thea Stilton and the Journey to the Lion's Den

Thea Stilton and the Great Tulip Heist

Thea Stilton and the Chocolate Sabotage

Thea Stilton and the Missing Myth